CW01177701

Two Sides of The Coin

By

Carla D E Godfrey

Chapter One

Staring into the bottom of an empty wine glass, knowing that there was plenty more where that came from was infinitely more preferable than what he had just come from. Twenty-two year old Daniel was still struggling the get the shrill like voice out of his ears. They had been seeing each other for about three months and yet he still couldn't really picture himself sharing a life with her.

'What do you mean you don't want us to move in together?'

'I just feel it's a bit soon...'

'A *bit* soon??? You think three months is a *bit soon?'* She was starting to go ultra-sonic by this point.

'I'm sorry Andrea but the answer's no!'

She glared at him and went white round the mouth before deliberately accidentally whacking him with her handbag and storming off. Lucky escape.

****

'I said can I get you another?'

He looked up to see a blonde haired young man smiling at him - he picked up his bottle. 'I'm alright thanks!'

'OK!' The man smiled and hopped on the stall next to him and gestured to the barman. 'So...what's a handsome guy like you doing sitting all by himself?'

'Well...If you must know...I'm toasting a lucky escape.'

'Oh really? Bunny boiler was she?'

'Something like that!'

'Hard luck!' He sipped his drink. 'I once went out with this guy - god! Talk about suffocating!'

Daniel frowned. 'How did you know I was straight?'

'No offence...but you just don't have...that quality!'

‘Right! Good to know!’

‘I’m Graham by the way!’

‘Daniel.’

‘So what do you do Daniel?’

‘I’m a broker.’

‘Oh? Clumsy are you?’

‘Very funny! What about you? Or are you a student?’

‘I’m an artist.’

‘Oh! One of those!’

‘”Oh! One of those!” I could do without the snide comments thank you very much!’

‘Any good?’

‘Well...I’d hardly be making any money at it if I wasn’t would I?’

Daniel grinned. 'Fair point.'

'Anyway! What about you? Dicing with death a bit aren't you?'

'How do you mean?'

'Well...if you lose your clients' money....'

'Hey! *They* make the decisions! I'm just the middle man - I mean I can offer advice but it's up to them if they take it!'

'Touché!' He looked at his watch. 'Midnight! You want to go on somewhere?'

Daniel laughed. 'Sorry! Not as carefree as I used to be!'

'Fine! Nice meeting ya!' Graham got up and started to walk away when he paused. 'Listen...I'm not coming on to you *at all!* But...well...you know, if you ever did feel like letting your hair down...well...here's my number.'

He looked at the number on his phone. ‘What would I want that for?’

‘Well...Just for the reason that I said!’

Daniel paused then he got out his mobile, copied the number and sent his. ‘Something tells me I’m going to regret this!’

‘You won’t! Promise!’ Then he was gone.

Chapter Two

Daniel didn't see Graham for the next three weeks - although he was still rather bemused at why they swapped numbers. The following days passed pretty uneventfully - And to be fair, he did get a lot of work done. Then, one day, out of the blue - he received a text.

"Drink?"

****

He was fully expecting another club - but - to his surprise - the name he was given lead him to a wine bar. He entered and then he noticed him - he was studying his phone.

'Hi!'

Graham looked up. 'Oh! Hi! Sorry! Just give me a minute.' He scrolled down a bit and then snapped it shut.

Daniel smiled. 'Sorry! Was I interrupting something?'

‘Nah! Just the ignorant wannabe’s who think they know it all!’

‘Sounds familiar!’

‘I got us a bottle.’

‘Thanks!’

‘So...’ Graham poured out a glass. ‘As this is our first date...’

‘Whoa! Slow down! This isn’t a “date!”

‘Of course not! So...Let’s keep it light on our first “date!”

Daniel shook his head. ‘Are you always this unapologetic?’

‘Why shouldn’t I be? Everyone should be proud of who they are.’

‘Very true!’

‘That’s why I got into art, to express my emotions! So...how about you?’

‘What about me?’

‘Well...anymore “lucky escapes?”

‘I think I’ll give the dating scene a rest for now!’

‘Fair enough!’

Daniel smiled. ‘What about you?’

‘Me?’

‘Yeah? Anyone special?’

‘Well...at the moment I’m chilling.’

‘Oh very American!’

Graham wrinkled his nose. ‘So...how do *you* relax, that’s assuming you’ve heard of that word!?’

Daniel raised his eyebrows. ‘I can relax! I normally just like a glass of wine and listen to music.’

‘Oh how very...boring!’

‘Well...at least I seem to have a more concrete direction in life!’

‘Oh! Ouch!’ Graham grinned. ‘I bet you’ve NEVER bunked off work have you?’

‘Have *you?’*

‘I’m an artist!’

‘Oh of course! Stupid question!’

‘What about you? Can’t be fun - stuck in an office...’

Daniel shrugged. ‘It pays the bills.’

Graham handed him a tenner. ‘If I give you some money - will you invest it for me?’

‘It doesn’t *quite* work like that!’

‘Oh? How does it work then?’

‘The going rate is about ten thousand pounds...’

‘Fucking hell!’

Daniel laughed.

‘What? You haven’t heard anyone swear before?’

‘Oh I’m *very* white collared!’

‘Clearly!’

Daniel frowned. ‘So...what exactly are you after? I may deal in money but that doesn’t mean I’m rolling in it!’

Graham shrugged. ‘Oh I don’t know! I like you!’

‘Nothing else?’

‘Well...it might be handy having an investor as a mate!’

He smiled. ‘Oh! I love being used!’

‘Who doesn’t?’ Graham lent forward. ‘Wanna know something?’

Daniel leant forward too, his heart

beating. ‘Oh?’

‘This is the best platonic date I’ve ever been on! Of course it’s the *only* platonic date I’ve been on!’

‘Well...as long as you don’t try to lead me astray...’

‘Perish the thought.’

Chapter Three

'Are you coming then?'

'I don't feel like it!'

'Oh come on Mate! it's been ages!'

Daniel looked at his friend squarely. 'Don't you think you're a little old for clubbing?'

'At twenty-two? Give over!'

'Whatever!' He picked up his phone again.

His friend grinned. 'That's the sixth time!'

'What?'

'That you've checked your phone. What's her name?'

'It's no-one! Just work!'

'Oh come on! Even I've noticed a change in you!'

'Meaning?'

'Well...you used to be quite solitary - now you seem more...animated!'

Daniel raised his eyebrows. 'Gee! Thanks!'

'So come on! What's her name?'

'It's no-one - trust me.'

****

Graham frowned as he watched the picture getting hung. 'A little to the left...' He took out his phone.

'Hello?'

'Hi! Daniel!'

'Oh...hi! Where have *you* been?'

'Well...believe it or not I've been busy - I usually fall off the radar at times anyway!'

‘Right!’

‘So...you’re calling me - I’m guessing you must be desperate...’

‘Far from it! I’m watching a large painting being hung - beats staring at a screen full of figures I bet!’

‘Touché! So...to what do I owe this pleasure?’

‘Well...I just thought you might want to come round to the gallery.’

‘When?’

‘Tonight.’

‘Oh? Is there a viewing on?’

‘No.’

‘Right...so why would I want to come along?’

‘I don’t know...I thought it might be an experience - being in an art gallery after closing.’

****

Daniel looked at the Monet and smiled - admiring the brushwork.

'You're a one for art then?!'

'I can appreciate it!'

Graham handed him a glass of wine and grinned. 'To tell you the truth; I'm still in training I mean this could be upside down for all I know!'

'Oh I'm sure that's not true!'

'It is! Trust me! My boss only hired me because she enjoyed my drawings and she took pity on me.'

'Well... I think you've done really well!' Daniel smiled. 'I have clients that like to invest in things like this.'

'Oh yeah? Couldn't throw any my way could you?'

'Oh? And we both benefit?'

‘Exactly!’

Daniel laughed. ‘I’ll try my best.’

Graham looked at his watch. ‘Oh well! Best think about closing up...’

‘Then on to a night club I suppose...’

‘God no! I’m not some kind of party animal!’

‘Oh you do surprise me!’

‘They do have the odd cheese and wine tasting evenings here.’

‘Well, I’m not surprised.’

Daniel looked around. ‘There’s something about being somewhere public after closing...’

‘Yeah! I agree!’ Graham suddenly turned to him. ‘Look...if I go AWOL - it’s nothing personal.’

‘I’ll bear that in mind!’

‘What do you think of this one?’

‘It’s beautiful.’

‘Yours for seven hundred!’

‘Fuck off!’

Chapter Four

I still don't understand it Darling!'

'What is there to understand?'

'He's straight!'

'What's that got to do with it?'

His friend shrugged. 'Well...I just thought…'

'What?'

'Well...it's not exactly going to go anywhere is it?'

Graham shook his head. 'This may come as a shock to you – but it *is* possible to be platonic!'

'Yes I know but if he was…'

'I don't know… I mean he *is* good looking!'

'Well...you never know!'

Graham laughed. 'Oh *please!* I'm good but I'm not *that* good!'

'What about this exhibition in Rome?'

'What about it?'

'Will you ask him to go with you?'

'Will you stop talking about him as if we were a couple!'

'Yeah but you like him right?'

'...Yes, yes I like him very much.'

****

At home… Graham stared at the e-mail again and again – it was telling him to confirm in the next two weeks if he was bringing someone or not. He reached for the phone but then thought better of it. Instead he texted him.

`Hey! What are you up to in the next four weeks?`

He didn't have to wait long.

Nothing much except work. Why do you ask?

Fancy a trip to Italy?

****

Daniel stared at it – he had to blink twice before replying.

????

There's a joint exhibition - my boss wants me to go over as a representative. I wondered if you'd like to come...

Are you allowed to bring people?

I've got two tickets if that helps.

Why me?

His answer took him by surprise.

I like you.

Then, as if he could read his mind.

`There'll be two separate rooms...don't worry.`

What made him reply with what he said next he didn't know.

`Who said I was worried? ;-)`

He immediately thought about backtracking but the reply told him that it was too late.

****

'You're going to *Italy??*'

Daniel shrugged 'It's just for a fortnight – he's going for his company's exhibition.'

His friend hesitated. 'Don't you think this is getting out of hand??'

'Hardly! There are two separate rooms!'

'Right! So when are you going to come out?'

‘Oh don’t be so absurd! This so isn’t what this is!’

‘Are you sure?’

‘Positive.’

****

After much thought, Daniel reached for the phone.

‘Hey!’

‘Hey!’

‘What’s up?’

‘Just one question’

‘Shoot.’

‘What *exactly* do you want me to come for?’

‘In all honesty - I have a spare ticket.’

‘So why not ask one of your friends?’

‘In all honesty - they’re not quite as...sophisticated.’

Daniel smiled. ‘Where as I can just take a week off at the drop of a hat!’

‘It’s only for a fortnight - very exclusive - two rooms, what do you say?’

Chapter Five

Daniel still didn't know what made him say yes - and he still felt as if he was in a trance as he started to pack everything. His head felt as if it was in a whirl - how the hell did they get here? Yet - it created a feeling of excitement in him that he couldn't explain. He seemed to represent everything that he wanted to be and more - and it was something that he thought that he could become dangerously addicted to.

****

'Flying?'

'Yeah! Couldn't be bothered to drive! You don't mind do you?'

'No! To be honest I Still can't believe I'm doing this!'

Graham grinned. 'Why? You never done anything crazy before?'

'Not on this scale no!'

‘It’ll be an experience.’

‘Oh it’ll certainly be that!’ He turned to him. ‘Why me?’

‘I’ve told you...I like you!’

‘Oh? And do you normally ask people you like to Italy?’

‘Not always! Sometimes it’s Germany!’

Daniel laughed.

‘Look, as I said - I had a spare ticket and I didn’t fancy taking anyone else.’

‘I’m honoured.’

They arrived and the hotel and checked in. Daniel looked around, taking in the design.

‘It’s something else isn’t it?’

‘Yeah! Don’t get me wrong but I was expecting something a little more...’

‘Modern?’ Graham laughed. ‘How many

more times? I am a professional!'

They headed to their rooms - Daniel smiled. 'What the hell am I doing here?'

'Because I asked you? Drink down at the bar, ten minutes?'

****

Daniel looked at himself in the mirror and took a deep breath. He had chosen to go smart casual. He had no idea why but he felt as if he was going on a date – utterly absurd.

He headed down to the bar.

'Wow! You look great!'

'Thanks!'

'What are you having?'

'Oh…I think I'll have a scotch.'

'Good idea!'

Daniel grinned. 'Don't tell me; the

company's paying.'

Graham laughed. 'Well…Up to a point!' He brought out a brochure. 'These are what I'm after!'

'They'll come out of your wages.'

'Yeah! Tell me about it!' He held up his glass. 'To a profitable time!'

'Cheers! Honestly! How desperate do you have to be to want someone to come with you?'

'Touché!

'I still don't really know why you invited me.'

'Because I like you and I hate to see people confined.'

'Who said I was confined?'

'Well…I just imagine you stuck to your desk in a stuffy environment.'

Graham smiled. 'Oh really? Yes, yes I

must admit that that's *just* what it's like.'

'Plus, I'm susceptible to handsome killjoys!'

'Gee thanks!'

'Well…look at you! You're *far* too serious! I bet you haven't done anything wild!'

'Might have mixed grape with the grain once and made myself seriously ill!'

Graham nearly choked, laughing. 'I stand corrected!'

'So…Are you all set?'

'Yep! Just about!' He hopped off the stool. 'Come on! Let's have a night cap in the room!'

Why not?!'

As they headed to their rooms - Daniel had no idea why he was suddenly feeling nervous - it was nervous energy - he had never felt so alive - Graham had given him something and he was becoming addicted to it.

'I could get used to this lifestyle!'

Graham went to the mini-bar. 'Many could!'

'Not meaning for this to sound...bad, but if I were you - I wouldn't want to share this with anyone!'

He grinned and came over to the bed. 'That's because you work with numbers and you're very generous!'

Daniel looked at him and immediately felt that same warm glow; it was a feeling he just couldn't explain but he knew that it was...pleasant and he didn't want to stop feeling it. 'Back to reality soon...'

'Why do you say that?'

'Because you can't live in a fantasy land forever.'

'No, but you can have a really good try!'

Daniel laughed. He hesitated - wondering whether or not to say the next bit. 'Thank you for prying me away from my desk - I-I've had a really good time!'

'Great! I mean I have to work but whatever!'

'Sorry! How's it going?'

'Yep! All wrapped up!' Graham brought out some champagne. 'Let's celebrate!'

Daniel raised his eyebrows. 'Wow! Your company is generous!'

'Sure! Especially when I pay myself!'

A moment later they lay on the bed next to each other but at a respectable distance. 'So this is what you're like when you let go!'

'You mean when I'm drunk?'

Graham faced him and stroked his cheek. 'You're not that drunk!'

Daniel felt the cool hand on his face and didn't bat it away. 'I'll let you know in the morning.'

Chapter Six

The following day, Daniel slowly opened his eyes and looked at the clock - it was quarter to eight. He looked and saw a couple of empty bottles and then saw Graham sleeping next to him. Fully dressed of course and on top of the bed. The auction had been a great success and Graham hadn't wanted the celebrating to end. To his surprise - he didn't freak out like he thought he would. Slowly, he rolled over onto his side and watched him sleep, he looked so peaceful. He felt an odd feeling of deep affection - what kind of affection he couldn't exactly make out, it was all new and confusing. He thought about their conversation the night before - he was like a jack-in-the-box, this was the first time he'd really seen him so relaxed - he took in the atmosphere, so quiet and still. Still feeling rather confused, yet immensely relieved that nothing had happened - he slowly got off the bed and went back to his room.

The shower was immensely refreshing - it was one of those rain showers that made you feel as if you were in a monsoon. Daniel closed his eyes as he felt the water fall on him, the cooling water was very welcoming - it almost took away his confused feelings. Was this getting out of hand?

'Morning!' Graham smiled a little shyly.

'Morning?'

'Guess we fell asleep!'

'Yes - yes we did.'

'Do you want to-'

'No.'

He nodded, a little disappointed. 'OK! Yeah! That's fair enough!'

They were staring at each other, each one desperately wanting the other to say something, to try and make things better in some way, to find a solution – but neither had the answer – and they knew it.

‘I’ll just get dressed.’

‘Yeah! And I’ll grab a shower.’

Daniel paused. ‘Thank you though - I have enjoyed it.’

Graham smiled. ‘Well...that’s something!’

****

There were still a few things to wrap up and then they were on their way home - they sat, next to each other as they had done coming except this time - Daniel was more acutely aware of the proximity between them.

Chapter Seven

Graham couldn't sleep - he was still thinking about what had happened between him and Daniel... had he misinterpreted it?

****

Daniel was busy - truth be told he was deliberately trying to be busy. For the first time in his life he was pleased to have a full inbox. He slowly realised that he had fallen into a sort of rabbit hole…at least that was what it seemed. He just felt so confused. He knew he wasn't gay and yet…when he was with him he felt so different. He felt happy and carefree which was more than he had felt in a long time. Up until recently – he had felt so sure of who he was – now…he just didn't really know anymore. He just knew that he didn't want it to stop and yet that in itself was unhealthy. He made a decision, he would have to pull back.

To tell the truth – he had yet to break the news to him – he had not heard a word from him all week – for which he had to be said, he was thankful, even though he knew that it was just delaying the inevitable.

That week turned into weeks and, at first, he was immensely relieved – he just got on with work, shopping, seeing friends and various other things in his life.

'Cheers mate!'

'Cheers!'

'It seems like forever since we've done this!'

'Yeah! I know…'

'I mean…what happened to you?'

Daniel shrugged. 'I…just got caught up with other projects that's all.'

'Well…you know what they say…all work and no play…'

'Oh it wasn't *all* work!'

‘Oh really?’ His friend grinned. ‘Go on…what’s her name?’

‘It…wasn’t like that…’

‘No – it never is mate.’

‘No…I mean it…it really wasn’t like that.’

‘Hey! None of my business mate!’

‘No…I just met this bloke…’

‘Oh? Dipping our toe in the pool are we?’

‘Oh behave! Not like that!’

‘Sorry…go on…’

‘No…he was just really nice and he opened my eyes to other stuff besides work.’

His friend laughed. ‘I’ve been trying to get you to do that for years! Well! Whoever this “mythical person” is – I’d like to shake his hand.’

'Yes!' If I ever see him again – Daniel thought.

Chapter Eight

Daniel was trying to ignore his mobile phone, but - with every ring - it was telling him that it was Graham desperately wanting his attention. He sighed and looked at his phone - and- to his disappointment - it wasn't Graham. Why hadn't he called him? It had been ages! The he shook himself - why the hell did he care if he called or not? If he ever called again or not... That was a thought... It would be best if he didn't maybe...this was getting for too complicated...how on earth did it come to this? He thought about it and it thought about it long and hard. The truth was - they were getting too attached. He wasn't gay! He knew that what worried him was if Graham got too comfortable and actually hoped for more. Even if he didn't...they seemed to be creating this emotional attachment to each other. Alright...it wasn't exactly romantic but the fact that he couldn't fully explain what it was frightened him. Throughout his life he had always been completely in control and then this kid showed up and, for some inexplicable reason - just made everything so much more complicated. How could he possibly have a healthy relationship with him when he couldn't even work out what it was? He hated to use the phrase but...in this context....he had been swept off his feet - it felt good - but it also felt unhealthy and was trying to pull him into a place that he knew nothing about - into the unknown. He wanted them to be friends but, the problem was...he wasn't sure what they were and, he knew that it sounded cliché to say that he wasn't gay but the truth was he really wasn't. Yet there was this inexplicable affection that stirred within him whenever he saw him. He just wanted to be with him... and that was what was making it unhealthy. Slowly, he reached for his phone.

'Hello?'

'Hi! Graham?'

'Oh Hi! How are you?'

'Fine!'

‘...You sure? You don’t sound fine?’

‘No...I am...Look, I think we need to talk.’

‘Oh? Don’t tell me - you want to repay the trip to Italy by dragging me to a boring conference in London...’

He laughed. ‘Not quite!’

‘Thank god! It would have been really hard to be polite I can tell you!’

‘No! It’s nothing like that!’

‘Phew!’

‘No...it-it’s a little closer to home...’

‘Oh?’

‘Yes...it’s about us.’

‘Us? Wait a minute...are you breaking up with me?’

‘Very funny!’

‘Is this to do with your worrying about what others think?’

‘Well...’

‘Because I’ve told you! We’re mates!’ He paused. ‘Best mates.’

Daniel didn’t answer.

‘Daniel? Aren’t we?’

‘Let’s just meet for lunch.’

‘Oh...OK! Saturday about one-ish?’

‘Saturday sounds perfect. See you then!’

Chapter Nine

Daniel looked at himself in the mirror and his heart sank. Why exactly was he doing this? Well...he knew exactly why he was doing this! Some would say it was an ego issue or an identity crises - that he wasn't comfortable in his own skin. Yet it really wasn't that - for the past few months he had felt as if he had disappeared down a rabbit hole and he hadn't wanted to move... he had forgone his friends, his other life - all to be sucked into another. He took a last look in the mirror, it wasn't going to be easy...but it had to be done.

****

It was a gorgeous, hot day - Graham had arranged to meet him outside the Cafe. He closed his eyes and drank in the sun that was beating on his face.

'Hi!'

'Oh hey! Just enjoying the sun!'

'Yes! I can see that!'

Graham removed his sunglasses. 'So...is everything OK? You sounded a bit serious.'

'Um...let's grab a drink first!'

'Fine!'

Soon, they were sipping cappuccinos.

Graham smiled. 'So...What did you want to tell me?'

Daniel cleared his throat. 'OK...I'm- I'm having a lot of fun...'

'Oh dear... This sounds like a break up!'

He laughed, but it was hollow. He then cleared his throat. 'Well...the thing is...I think...well...I think it would be healthy...for both of us if we took a step back...'

'From what?'

'From this...'

'Oh right! OK! Mate!'

'No...I'm serious...'

Graham stared at him. 'But I-I don't understand...'

'It's not you it's me...'

'Look...it's fine! I get it! When I first discovered I was gay my head was all over the place...'

'Woah! Hey! What are you on about? I'm not gay!'

'Really?'

'Yes! I'm pretty sure I'd know by now!'

Graham scrutinised him. 'Yeah... probably right... Like I said, you don't seem to have that...quality!'

'Again...thanks!'

'So...what's the problem?'

'I just...I don't think...I think we should just give each other some space...'

'Why?'

'Well....I...there's a lot going on...I'm not even sure how I feel.'

'But...you just said...'

'I know...I know what I said...'

Graham looked at him. 'I-I'm not contagious you know! I'm not going to pass my "gayness" on to you!'

'No! I know that but...I'm addicted - I...don't know what's going on and...until I do...I just think that this is unhealthy.'

They stared at each other in pure silence. Graham, calmly sipped his coffee. 'Well...there you go...' He got up to leave. 'I only ever wanted to be a good friend to you.'

'Graham-'

'No! I maybe a lot younger than you but that does not make me naive! Maybe yes! Maybe I would have liked something to happen between us - but you can't be what you're not and, believe it or not I am mature enough to understand that. But, clearly you don't think I'm capable!'

'Graham wait...'

He got up. 'Goodbye Daniel...It was nice knowing you.'

And just like that, Daniel watched him walk out of his life.

Chapter Ten

Daniel wasn't expecting to come crashing down as hard as he did - Graham had really opened his eyes to a different life outside work. The problem was - it had also started to stir other feelings in him - he was so enthusiastic and full of life - it was quite addictive. These new feelings frightened him and, until, he figured out what they were - he thought it best to steer clear. For the next few weeks - he threw himself into work, knowing that it was to try and help him to forget more than anything else. It was for the best. He actually managed to catch up a lot with his own life; he worked hard and caught up with his friends. Soon, things went back to how they used to be. However, it didn't change the fact that whenever the phone went - his heart leapt, only for it to sadly return to its normal place in his chest.

****

'Still nothing?'

'No.'

‘I don’t understand what the big deal is...are you..?’

‘Oh for god’s sake! How many more times??’

‘No- alright fine!’ His friend sipped his coffee. ‘But...I don’t understand, you’re the one who said that you should take a break from each other?’

‘Yeah!’

‘Why exactly?’

Daniel fell silent. ‘I...I don’t really know...it’s just getting....complicated.’

‘Complicated how?’

‘I don’t know!’

‘Well....what does it feel like?’

‘I don’t know!’

‘You don’t know how you feel?’

‘Well...I do but it’s hard to explain...’

‘Well...try...’

‘I don’t know...it’s like...I’ve fallen in love with him...platonically. He makes me feel everything except the sexy part...does that make sense?’

‘I think so...’

‘Oh I don’t know...’

‘Why don’t you talk to him about it?’

‘No...The last thing I want to do is lead him on...I just think we need to give each other space.’

His friend sipped his drink. ‘Well...it’s up to you mate.’

‘It’s for the best...there’s nothing going on.’

‘OK! I believe you!’

‘It’s the truth!’

‘OK!’

Chapter Eleven

Six months later...

'Congratulations Graham! You must be thrilled!'

'Thanks!'

'These pictures are stunning!'

'Thank you!'

Graham was throwing an exclusive opening for his latest exhibition and it was going well. It was true that Daniel was never far from his mind - but that was door that had been firmly shut a while ago it seemed.

'Hey!'

He smiled as he saw his friend. 'Robin! Good to see you!'

'Hello! Congratulations!'

‘Thank you!’

‘How are you?’

‘Fine! Never better! You?’

‘Can’t complain!’ He grabbed a glass of champagne. ‘Yeah! Life’s good! And, just for the record, I can still work out when you’re lying...’

‘I don’t know what you mean!’

‘You know exactly what I mean! You miss him don’t you?’

‘We weren’t a couple Rob!’

‘No I realise that! But there are all sorts of relationships Graham!’

‘I don’t know...’

‘Look...if he makes you feel happy...what does it matter?’

‘That’s not the issue...He won’t talk to me until he figures out what it is.’

‘Well...don’t wait around too long otherwise he won’t be worth it. Don’t put yourself down, show your worth.’

****

That night, Graham lay on his bed, staring at Daniel’s phone number. He missed him.

****

He was afraid, he knew that it was a bit of a cliché, a man afraid of his emotions and - he knew that he should be pleased that he’d got everything sorted in his mind but the truth was...he wasn’t. He wasn’t some teenager who was afraid what others thought of him - he didn’t particularly care if people thought he was gay or not - he just hated not being able to define something - he would be the last to admit that he was afraid - yet, it could be argued that, as he was not confronting his feelings, as he was just running away and avoiding Graham - that equally made him a coward - a confrontation was awaiting him... whether he liked it or not.

Chapter Twelve

Graham opened his eyes the following morning - he had been out the night before...clubbing, normally, after a big exhibition he liked to blow off some steam. It was a Sunday so he knew that he didn't have any work. He lay back and thought about how well it had gone. He thought again about Daniel, He had completely fallen in love with him; it wasn't a normal love - it seemed to be teetering between the romantic and the platonic - but the result was the same - he was in love with him, but it was over...Daniel had made that perfectly clear - so he would stay away…

****

Daniel slowly poured out his coffee; he wasn't looking forward to what he was about to do, but the truth was this friendship was messing with his head. That's why he had needed to put a stop to it, before he fell in too deep - that's all he had been trying to do.

****

He was more than surprised to see that Graham was waiting for him at his office the following day.

'What are you doing here?'

'We have to talk about this!'

'There's nothing to talk about!'

Graham followed him into his office. 'Bullshit! Why can't you just be honest??'

Daniel looked at him and laughed. 'What the hell do you think is going on here?'

'I don't know! Neither do you! That's what scares you!'

'Yes!' He banged the desk. 'Yes! You're right! It does scare me! I-I can't stop thinking about you - I'm always looking forward to seeing you - but I'm not gay!'

'Who is saying you are?'

'I'm not saying...'

Graham shook his head. 'I can't believe how immature you are!'

'That's not the problem! As I've said; I don't want you to get the wrong idea...'

'...And as I've said - I know you're not gay! I just love being with you!'

'It's not...'

'Not what? It feels right! Why can't you understand that? And you know it!'

'This has to stop now!'

Graham glared at him. 'Fine! If that's how you *really* feel.' Then he was gone.

Chapter Thirteen

Daniel had hoped that the work would continue forever - when he was busy - he wasn't thinking about the way he had ended things with Graham. Not that he particularly regretted it but it was the way that it had been handled. That could have been done more sensitively he acknowledged that but, the truth was he didn't want to own up to the fact that he was scared. Scared of his feelings, scared of finding out whatever this was.

****

Graham was keeping busy - he was just replying to an e-mail confirming his trip to New York; he would be gone for six months. He was considering spending Christmas there as well; it would be nice to see Rockefeller's Christmas tree.

****

Daniel poured himself another drink, he needed the courage for what he was about to do. He knew that he had treated him horribly - but - the truth was; he missed him. Every time the phone went, he had hoped that it would be him and had been disappointed when it wasn't. He phoned him again.

'Hello?'

'Hey!'

There was a pause. 'Hey!'

'How are you?'

'I'm fine! How are you?'

'Yeah! Not bad!'

'Busy?'

'Yeah! You?'

'Yeah! Can't complain.'

'Hey! Listen about last time…'

'Forget it!'

'No I shouldn't have…'

‘No…It’s me I overreacted.’

‘Well…for what it’s worth I’m still sorry.’

‘Me too.’

There was another pause, this conversation was so awkward. ‘I was thinking about Christmas time...’

‘Christmas???’

‘Yeah I know! It’s ages away!’

‘What about it?’

‘Well... I’ve got to oversee a new project.’

‘Oh! Good for you!’

‘It’s in New York...’

Daniel fell silent.

‘Daniel?’

‘New York? Wow!’

‘Yeah! Pretty big!’

‘So...you’ll be gone for six months?’

‘About that...yes! Maybe longer.’

Daniel felt a lump in his throat.’ Wow! That’s great! I’m really pleased for you.’

‘Hey! We’ll keep in touch!’

‘Yes! Absolutely!’

****

That night, both lay awake, just staring at the ceiling.

Chapter Fourteen

The sun shone - it was a glorious hot day in June, Daniel looked at his watch - Graham would be taking off by now. He suddenly felt an innate sense of calmness - it was for the best. Then, to his immense annoyance - a wave of tears suddenly washed over him, he swallowed hard and forced the urge away. Instead, he threw himself into getting back in touch with what was going on in his own life. He caught up with his friends, he caught up on work - in fact, it felt like - at least to him - that he was deliberately drowning himself in work and his life to try and forget. Suddenly, he heard his phone ping.

`Wish you were here!`

He stared at the text and felt a warm, tingling feeling, he texted back.

`Good luck with everything! Enjoy!`

No sooner had he sent it then he felt that re-occurring lump in his throat; still, he refused to give in to his feelings - despite his reaction - he told himself that he wouldn't lose any sleep over it if he never saw him again.

****

Friday night - Daniel sat at the bar, just staring at his drink.

'You're missing him aren't you?'

'Robin - I don't want to talk about it!'

'Oh for god's sake! Why don't you just go out and join him?'

'What the hell for???'

'Because it's obvious you miss him!'

'It is not obvious! Anyway I can't!'

'Why can't you?'

'Because I'm busy working!'

His friend shook his head. 'I don't know what's going on here - but all I know is I noticed a change in you - and if he is the reason for this change, then you shouldn't let that go - whatever it is, just go and sort it out.'

****

Back home, Daniel stared at the text and then looked at his e-mail, he opened a new e-mail and stared at the blank screen, unable to think about what to write. Instead - he just turned off his computer - there was nothing to say.

****

Graham looked out at the hot sunshine - he decided to give it one more go, he sent a text.

`Come and join me.`

Chapter Fifteen

Daniel waited and waited, suddenly, Graham answered.

'Hey!'

'Hey!'

He smiled. 'Well! A video call! I am honoured!'

Daniel felt his heart tying up into knots. 'How's it going?'

'Fine!'

'Great.'

There was a pause. 'Did you get my message?'

'...Yeah...Yeah I got it.'

'Well?'

Daniel swallowed hard. 'Graham - I don't regret a single second of meeting you...'

‘I know you think it’s best to put some distance between us...’

‘Yeah I know!’

‘Daniel...what do you want? Why are you calling me?’

‘I don’t really know...’

There was another pause. ‘Come out and join me.’

‘What?’

‘You heard!’

‘Graham...’

‘Daniel...Listen - it’s obvious that you want to talk.’

‘We don’t have anything left to say...’

‘Oh come on! That’s rubbish and you know it!’

‘What are you suggesting?’

‘I’m suggesting that you come out and join me - did you not hear me the first time??’

‘Yes but I can’t...’

‘Can’t...or won’t?’

‘What difference does it make???’

‘Please...it’s very important.’

‘What’s so important that you can’t tell me now?’

‘I’d rather tell you face to face...’

‘Well...I can’t come at the moment...’

‘No rush...When you can.’

Chapter Sixteen

Daniel looked at his passport - at first, he thought it would be best to do all of this over the phone - he just didn't have the strength to do it face to face. Maybe this would be the perfect way to say good-bye.

****

Getting off the plane - Daniel was struck by how intimidating it all was. He looked out at the city and felt a bit like Kevin McAllister in Home Alone 2. It really was something - he couldn't deny that. He texted Graham to let him know he had arrived. Graham texted him back an address.

'Wow!'

'What do you think?'

Daniel looked around the apartment. 'Not bad!'

‘It isn’t is it? I mean it maybe a little pokey but I’m only renting...for the moment anyway...’

‘What do you mean “for the moment?”

‘Oh...Well...You know...I might grow to like it round here. Wine?’

‘Thanks.’ He looked around. ‘Well...Yeah! I could see that.’ He felt numb. ‘But what about your family?’

‘They could visit.’

‘Yes...they could...’

‘Well...As I said...I’m just thinking about it.’

‘Well...No doubt it’s a great opportunity.’ Daniel looked out the window. ‘So...just out of pure curiosity...after all this is over...do you think that you would be happy?’

‘I’m a big boy! I can handle living on my own!’

'No I realise that! It's just in...a foreign country...'

'Well...We do speak the same language!'

'Sure! Well...It's a great opportunity for you! I'm pleased for you!'

'Thanks!'

Daniel sipped his drink. 'Remember me when you're rich and famous!'

'Well...I certainly will do my best!'

'Very funny!' He quickly turned away as he felt the tears rise up.

'Hey! Hey!' Graham gripped his shoulder. 'We'll keep in touch!'

'Yes, of course!'

'Unless...'

'Unless what?'

'Well...unless you stay here with me?'

He stared at him. ‘Jesus! You are relentless!’

Graham grinned. ‘You’re tempted though aren’t you?’

‘No!’

He sat in front of him and took his hands in his. ‘Not even a little bit?’

‘Graham I’m not going to uproot my entire life for you!’

‘Fine! Just thought I’d ask...’

‘You’re impossible! You know that?!’

‘Just look at that view!’

Daniel looked, it was something. ‘Look...I’m really happy for you and we can e-mail and do face time.

‘Yeah I know but it’s not the same is it?’

‘...No it’s not...’

‘I don’t know about you but that view for me puts everything into perspective.’

‘Meaning?’

Daniel shrugged. ‘Just that!’

Chapter Seventeen

For the next few weeks Daniel and Graham were inseparable - One evening while they were preparing dinner. Graham grinned.

'You're the best date I've ever had!'

'Gee! Thanks for that!' Daniel opened the wine. 'Graham...listen...we have to talk.'

'Oh dear! Here we go again!'

'No! It's not like that...'

'But it is! You're feeling insecure again!'

'Maybe but...honestly the reason is...' He took a deep breath. 'I don't ever want this to end - you make me feel so alive and...I think I'm in love with you...'

He raised his eyebrows. 'But I thought you said...'

‘Oh no! No! I-I don’t mean I’m *romantically* in love with you but...the way you make me feel! You’re the best friend I’ve ever had!’

‘OK...So what does that mean?’

Daniel felt the tears form in his eyes. ‘It-it means I-I don’t want us to ever lose sight each other...’

Graham began to smile. ‘Dear god! What’s got into you?’

‘I don’t know! I- I just love how you make me feel.’

‘What? Not a stuffy shirt?’

‘Exactly!’

Graham bit his lip. ‘You know... I just love how sophisticated you are!’

‘Me? Sophisticated?’

‘Well...yes! You’re so together and you’ve got it all figured out.’

‘Well...You have a massive zest for life!’

‘So...why can’t we just enjoy what we have and mix our personalities together? Because...I love you too.’

Daniel looked at him and felt more sure than he ever had.

Chapter Eighteen

Waking up the following morning - Daniel knew that he had to tell him the truth; he had given him one last night together - and that would be the end of it.

Walking into the kitchen, Graham smiled. 'Hey! Coffee?'

'Thanks!'

'How's your head?'

'Well...I'm embarrassed to admit that it's been a while since I've drunk that much!'

He smiled. 'You were letting your hair down!'

'Yes! Can't do it too often though.'

'Why not? Oh! I forget! Responsibilities!'

'Yes... Among other things...'

'OK! Out with it! What is it?'

Daniel paused. ‘Well...I-I just wanted to say...I think it’s great that you’re moving to New York.’

‘Yeah? You’ll come and visit...’

‘Ummm...Graham...Like I said - I think this would be a brilliant idea to look at this as a fresh start.’

‘What’s that supposed to mean? Because you’re afraid of your feelings - we can’t be friends?’

‘It isn’t like that!’

‘Oh no? What is it like then?’

Daniel stared at him. ‘I...I don’t know...’

‘Really? Because it just feels like we’re going round in circles.’ Graham put his cup down and went up to him. ‘There are all kinds of love and the love we share is deep but it is platonic and I’m alright with that...’

Daniel rested his forehead against his without saying a word, but that was OK...he didn't have to.

'So? You will come and visit me then?'

'Just try and stop me.'

'That's better!'

'OK! OK! I admit it - I'm going to miss you.'

'I'll miss you too.'

A wave of relief once again washed over him, he was pleased to finally be able to let him go and yet keep hold of him at the same time. He was also glad that they had got everything out in the open and established their relationship at the same time; it was the perfect way to say good-bye.

Chapter Nineteen

If Daniel thought that was the end of his chapter with Graham then he was about to be mistaken; it had barely been a couple of months since they had said good bye and, even then, Daniel found himself still looking at his phone as though willing it to ring. It didn't. He had to face up to the fact that it truly was the end. He let out his breath slowly, he wasn't entirely sure whether or not to be relieved.

****

One evening, he was looking through some papers when his phone went, he smiled as he saw who it was.

'Hey you!'

'Hey!'

'Can I just ask you something?'

'Of course!'

'You can say no...'

Daniel's heart leapt. 'What is it Graham? I'm not moving out there with you if that's what you're after!'

He laughed. 'God forbid! You'd cramped my style!'

'Oh! Thanks! What is it then?'

'Well...I was just wondering...how about we meet up every six months or so?'

'How do you mean?'

'Well...why should we just limit it to e-mails and texts?'

Daniel felt the familiar chill rush down his back. 'Only every six months?'

He laughed. 'Trust me! That will fly by! You don't need me there...cramping your style.'

'Why suggest it then?'

There was a pause. 'Because I never ever want to lose touch with you again. Now that we've-'

'We've?'

'"Declared our undying love to each other!'

'Very funny!' Daniel smiled. 'You know...I reckon I'd have a much better deal - flying out there to see you.'

Graham laughed. 'Is that right?? Well…yes you have a point!'

'Gee…thanks!'

'Hey! You lay yourself open for that mate!'

True!' there was a pause. 'So…'

'Wait! That's...not just the reason...'

'Oh?'

Daniel sighed. 'The truth is...I miss you too...'

'Say that again...'

'You heard…I should have said this to you ages ago.'

'Well...you kinda did...'

'No I didn't...not properly...The truth is, I was struggling to work out what our relationship was and that frightened me.'

'Yes...I know how you like to be in control!'

'Not at all! I just like knowing where we stand...'

'And where is that exactly Daniel?'

Daniel paused. 'Let's meet for one last drink.'

'OK...I thought we already did that though.' He paused. '...OK. Let's do it.'

Chapter Twenty

Daniel looked out of the taxi as it pulled up outside Graham's flat.

'You made it then!'

'It's quite something this place isn't it?'

'You can say that again! Drink?'

'Thanks!' Daniel bit his lip. 'So...this thing we have to talk about...'

'I think I know what you're going to say...'

'This is a perfect opportunity to make a clean break...'

He nodded, trying not to cry. 'I see...'

'This is nothing to do with you...it's me...I-I love being with you but...I- I sort of feel that I'm disappearing down a rabbit hole.'

'How do you mean?'

‘I’m afraid that I’ll lose touch with reality, it’s not healthy!’

‘What you mean is you’re afraid to enjoy yourself!’

‘Well...I wouldn’t put it quite like that!’

‘Really? I would!’ Graham put his glass down. ‘Daniel...I’ve told you - there’s nothing to be afraid of - you’re still doing your work alright - what we have is unique - a really good friendship and...I’m glad I found you - I love you.’

Daniel’s eyes widened, but he didn’t feel like denying it, instead he picked up his glass and touched Graham’s. ‘I-I have been wrapped up in work for so long that I’ve forgotten how to live - in fact I didn’t even care. Even my friends didn’t touch the sides.’

‘...And that’s my fault I suppose?’

‘Oh you bet!’

‘You don’t have to lose “touch with reality” as you so dramatically put it, I honestly didn’t realise that I had so much power!’

‘So...what are you proposing?’

‘...That I be your breath of fresh air?’

‘Meaning?’

He shrugged and suddenly came over shy. ‘I don’t know just...if you need to breathe or to let off some steam - we’d make a great duo you and me.’

‘Like a comedy duo?’

‘Well...like... whatever you like!’

Daniel looked at Graham, felt the same warm feeling and liked it. He slowly reached for his hand.

Chapter Twenty-One

The days seemed to go so fast and, before he knew it, it was time for him to go home. They had been inseparable and he had really enjoyed himself. Yet now, it was time for him to take a deep breath - it was the perfect end.

Graham watched him pack. 'I've had a really good time you know.'

'Me too.'

'So...' He sat on the edge of the bed. 'Where do we go from here?'

There it was...the question that Daniel was dreading. He sighed and stopped packing, he sat down next to him. 'I think we should start as we mean to go on.'

'What does that mean exactly?'

'It means that - finally- I can accept the fact that I want you in my life, that I need you in my life.'

'Really?'

'Yes! I want to receive your texts, your messages, I want it all Graham. 'He smiled at him. 'I'm just so sorry that it took me so long to realise it.'

'Do you? Do you really?'

'Yes!'

Graham smiled and slowly reached for his hand. 'I mean it you know, you're the best friend I've ever had!'

Daniel laughed. 'God! You must be desperate!'

'No! I'm serious!'

'Well...you've taught me how to not be so...'

'Stuck up? Stuffy?'

'Among other things, thanks!'

Graham placed a hand on his shoulder. 'Out of all the stuck up, stuffy people I've met; I can reassure you that there are worse!'

'Gee...thanks!'

'So...when we come back down to earth...'

'Look, I want to in my life - I need you in my life.'

'...To stop you self-destructing?'

'Among other things.'

'You and me against the world?'

Daniel smiled and squeezed his hand. 'You and me against the world.'

Chapter Twenty-Two

Graham felt so happy! He felt that he had truly met his soul mate - it may be platonic - but, in this space and time - that was all he needed.

****

Daniel smiled to himself all the way home - he was still trying to come back down to earth - he slowly realised how stupid he'd been - he had been so busy trying to define what it was that he had forgotten that it was more important to accept it for what it was. He knew who he was and he knew what he wanted, the way he wanted Graham was unique and it suited them both.

Chapter Twenty-Three

Daniel was feeling nervous although he really had no idea why - he looked at his watch, Graham would be here any minute. He was over for an exhibition and had wanted to stop by.

Suddenly, there was a knock at the door. He looked tired. 'God! The journey!'

'Yeah! Tell me about it! Come in!'

Graham grinned. 'Call me a jerk but everything seems smaller now!'

'You're a jerk!'

'Funny!'

Daniel bit his lip. 'I'm really glad you're here you know!'

'Oh? Then how come you haven't offered me a drink?'

He laughed. 'Touché!'

'Thanks!'

‘I’m glad you’re here!’

‘...And I’m glad to be here! Although...you’re going to have more of a holiday than I am when you come to visit!’

‘Oh I’m so sorry!’

‘So you should be!’ Graham sipped his drink. ‘So...how do you feel about it?’

‘About what?’

‘You know what!’

Daniel smiled. ‘ Well...I can’t keep coming over all the time! It does cost!’

‘Every four months?’

‘I will try to make it every four but it may occasionally stretch to six!’

‘...And in the mean time! We can face time!’

‘Exactly!’

‘There is one other solution...’

‘No! No Graham! I can’t move out there!’

‘Why not! What’s stopping you?!’

‘My job for one! It’s a nice idea but I just can’t!’

‘Oh well! Worth a try!’

Daniel shook his head. ‘What the hell are you doing to me? Before you I wouldn’t even consider a holiday!’

‘Yes! I figured!’ Graham cocked his head. ‘Hey! Hey! What is it?’

‘Nothing! Don’t be absurd!’ Daniel was embarrassed to feel the tears prick his eyes.

‘Come on! We can do this! I’m calling it! Every five months!’

‘Every five months.’

Graham squeezed his hands reassuringly.

Chapter Twenty-Four

'Are you asleep?'

'No.'

Graham slowly opened his bedroom door and slipped in, he sat on his bed.

Daniel raised his eyebrows. 'Thank you for wearing your dressing gown!'

'Hey! What do you take me for?'

'Do you really want me to answer that?'

Daniel smiled. 'Jet lag?'

'Oddly enough...no. I was thinking about when you come over again.'

'Steady on! You've only just got here!'

'Yeah! I know! But just think! We could have a good thing going you and me!'

'Yeah... we could.'

'So...'

‘I can’t keep taking time off work!’

‘Who’s suggesting that?’

‘You are!’

‘Hardly!’

‘Oh yeah? Then what’s with the smile?’

‘Well...OK, maybe a little...’

Daniel smiled. ‘Alright! I’ll tell you what...I will come over for every exhibition that you have!’

Graham grinned. ‘In that case I’d best have a lot of them!’

‘Don’t get cocky!’

‘Just saying!’

Daniel took his face in his hands and rested his forehead against his.

‘Honestly! What am I to do with you?’

‘Answers on a postcard please!’

Chapter Twenty-Five

It was midnight when the two of them came crashing in.

'That was amazing! Congratulations!'

'Well! That's how you give an exhibition!' Graham threw himself down on the sofa.

'Hey! Careful!'

'Sorry!'

Daniel shook his head. 'Drink?'

'Yeah! Why not! Let's celebrate!'

'I'm really, really pleased for you Graham! Cheers!'

'Thanks!'

Daniel handed him a glass of champagne. 'To a successful career!'

'A successful career!'

‘So! I don’t envy you the flight back!’

‘Oh well! Needs must!’

Daniel sipped his champagne. ‘My turn next time!’

‘I’ll hold you to that!’

‘Cheers!’

‘Cheers!’

‘Still - there is one solution...’

‘No! I’m not moving out there I’ve told you that before!’

‘Oh damn!’

Daniel laughed. ‘You’re persistent...I’ll give you that!’

‘Yeah! And you’re stubborn!’

‘Oh just because I won’t uproot my entire life for you!’

'Can't have much fun if we're on opposite sides of the world!'

'You're never going to grow up are you?'

'God! I hope not!'

Daniel smiled. 'I'm really pleased for you! You've really landed on your feet!'

'Well...That's not much good if you're not here to celebrate with me!'

'You're doing it again!'

'Doing what?'

Daniel tapped him on the head. 'Emotionally blackmailing me!'

Graham tried to look innocent. 'Moi?!'

'Yes! "Toi!"'

'Oh Daniel!!' He threw himself down on the bed. 'What are we to do?'

'Stop being such a drama queen!'

‘You’re right!’

Daniel laughed. ‘What the hell are you doing now?’

Graham turned round with another bottle. ‘Getting some more champagne...what does it look like?’

Chapter Twenty-Six

The following morning - Daniel couldn't even open his eyes, the sun poured through and he pulled the quilt over his head. Finally, summoning the strength, he dragged himself out of bed and headed towards the kitchen.

'Morning!'

He watched as Graham grabbed two cups. 'Coffee?'

'Oh yes! Please! help yourself!'

'Sorry!'

He laughed. 'No worries!'

'You know, some would say we needed tomato juice, raw eggs and Tabasco...'

'Vomit the hangover away, there's a thought!'

'Very funny!'

‘If it’s all the same to you...I think I’ll stick with coffee!’

‘Can’t blame you to be honest!’ Graham handed him a cup.

‘How can you be so peppy?’

He shrugged. ‘Younger?’

‘Ouch! Thank you for that!’

‘You’re welcome!’

Daniel sipped his drink and shivered, the eggs and tomato juice was bitter yet the Tabasco gave it a kick which seemed to snap him out of it.

‘Well?’

‘Not bad! Thanks! But I won’t be doing this for a while!’

‘Best not...at your age...’

‘Ouch again! I’m not that much older than you!’

‘True!’

‘I suppose you’ll be glad to get back to reality!’

‘You can say that again! When you come over we definitely won’t be doing this!’

‘Ah! On your turf then!’

‘Exactly!’

‘Then I think I won’t bother!’

‘Charming!’

‘Well...anything can happen in four months!’

‘True!’

‘Cheers!’ Daniel touched his cup with his.

‘Cheers.’

‘So...your moving out there is still a no?!’

‘Absolutely!’

‘Well...there’s always renting...’

‘Graham!’

‘Sorry! Sorry!’

Chapter Twenty-Seven

'It's a shame it's all over.' Daniel joined Graham in the gallery as his paintings were packed away.

'I know! But there's always next year!'

'I'll come out to you next time.'

'Promise?'

'I promise!'

'That'll be fun!'

Daniel laughed, he looked sideways at his friend and felt a pang. 'I don't want you to go...'

Graham smiled. 'I don't want to go either.'

'Still...'

'Still! I may have to return - but it doesn't mean that our adventure is over!'

'Adventure?'

‘Yes! We’ve been on an adventure ever since we first met!’

‘Yes!’ Daniel laughed. ‘I suppose we have!’

‘...And there is absolutely no reason why it should stop...just because we’re on the opposite sides of the world!’

‘Of course not! There’s always e-mail and text...’

‘Oh trust you to be boring!’

‘I’m just saying! I certainly can’t afford regular trips!’

‘I’ll pay!’

‘No you bloody won’t!’

He laughed. ‘Worth a try!’

‘What’s next?’

‘In the art world? Who knows?’

'Hey! This may be the start of some-thing!'

'What...you mean this year Ameri-ca...next year the world?!'

'Exactly!'

'Hardly!'

Daniel smiled. 'Graham, you brought me out of my shell and I'll always be grate-ful for that!'

'You didn't need much persuading.'

'Well...maybe I just needed reminding.'

'Come with me.'

'Why?'

'I want to show you something.'

Daniel frowned. 'Aren't they going to close?'

'In a minute! I want to show you some-thing.' He led him to a picture.

‘One of yours?’

‘Yes! Look at it.’

Daniel studied the painting; it consisted of two men and a door but with two completely different sceneries behind them.

‘Anything’s possible...’

‘Anything’s possible.’ Daniel was suddenly aware of the gallery being very empty - it was just them, the only two left in the world, slowly, he reached for Graham’s hand and gave it a squeeze as he continued to admire and study the brushwork.

Fin

www.ingramcontent.com/pod-product-compliance
Ingram Content Group UK Ltd.
Pitfield, Milton Keynes, MK11 3LW, UK
UKHW042056131224
452457UK00004B/285

9 798227 333995